MR. MEAN

by Roger Hargreaves

WORLD INTERNATIONAL

Mr Mean lived up to his name.

He lived in what could have been a nice house, but wasn't.

He never painted it, or mended the windows, or repaired the roof.

Inside it was the same.

No carpets! No curtains! No pictures! No fires!

And Mr Mean was so mean he made his furniture out of old orange boxes, and then complained about the price of nails!

Why, he was so mean, do you know what he gave his brother for Christmas last year?

A piece of coal!

It wasn't as if Mr Mean didn't have any money.

Oh no!

He had lots of money, and he kept it all hidden in a box which he kept in the kitchen.

Every evening, he'd sit there counting it. It was the only thing Mr Mean liked doing.

But would he spend it?

Oh dear me, no.

Not old Meany.

Not if he could help it!

One day, Mr Mean was sitting in his gloomy kitchen having a gloomy meal.

He only ever had one meal a day, and that day, he was having a cup of water and a piece of bread which was three weeks old.

Suddenly, he was interrupted by a knock at the door.

"Drat!" he said, because he didn't like people. "Drat and bother!"

He opened the door, and there, on his doorstep, stood a wizard.

A rather fat wizard.

"Hello," said the wizard. "I wonder if, by any chance, as it's such a warm day, you could possibly, if it's not too much trouble, be so kind as to, if it's not inconvenient, perhaps, as I'm very thirsty, provide me with, do you think, a glass, if it's not too much to ask, of water, please?"

He was a very wordy wizard.

"No!" replied Mr Mean rudely, and shut the door in his face.

And went back into his kitchen to finish his meagre meal.

But there, standing in front of him, was the wizard.

"How did you get in?" gasped Mr Mean.

"Well," replied the wizard, "it was by, how shall I put it, I just, well, you know, waved the old whatsitsname, magic wand don't you know, and, well, here I am, if you know what I mean!"

"You must be very poor," he remarked kindly, looking around.

"Oh, yes I am," lied Mr Mean.

"Then perhaps I can help you," said the wizard, pulling up a box to sit down on.

The box didn't move, so the wizard pulled it harder, and this time it did move. In fact it tipped up and spilled all Mr Mean's money all over the floor.

"Well well well," exclaimed the wizard, eyeing the money rolling all over the kitchen floor. "Well well well well well well!"

"It would appear to me," he continued, "that you, sir, are an old Meany!"

Mr Mean didn't hear him.

He was too busy scrabbling all over the floor trying to pick up his money.

"And meanies," added the wizard, "need to be taught a lesson!"

So saying, he waved his magic wand.

All the money turned into potatoes!

Potatoes!

Poor Mr Mean.

"Oh! Oh dear! Oh dear me!" he wailed. "Please turn my money back into money. Oh please, please,please," he begged.

"Perhaps," replied the wizard. "But, on the other hand, taking all things into account, by and large, things being what they are, on the face of it, perhaps not."

"However," continued the wordy wizard, "if you make me a solemn promise never to be mean again, then I will turn your money back into money. But," he added sternly, "if you are ever mean again, then it's, how can I put it, then it's potatoes for you my lad. If not other vegetables as well!"

Then the wizard had the glass of water he'd come for in the first place, except it was a cup of water because Mr Mean didn't have any glasses.

Then, with another wave of his wand, he turned the potatoes back into money, and another wave of his wand made himself disappear.

"Stupid wizard," muttered Mr Mean, picking up all his money.

The following day, Mr Mean decided to walk to town.

He never took the bus because that cost money!

On the way, he met an old washerwoman carrying an enormous bundle of washing.

"Please kind sir," she asked, "could you possibly help me to carry this washing? It's so heavy!"

"No!" replied Mr Mean. "It's your washing. You carry it!"

But, as soon as he'd said that, he felt a tingling in his nose.

Mr Mean's nose turned into a carrot!!

"Oh no!" he gasped.

The old washerwoman chuckled.

And then Mr Mean remembered the wizard's words.

"Yes! Yes!" he cried in a panic. "Of course I'll help you!"

And he carried the huge bundle of washing to where the old washerwoman wanted.

And the carrot turned back into a nose, and off he went.

The old washerwoman chuckled again, and turned back into the wizard.

It had been him all along!

On his way into town, Mr Mean passed by a cottage garden.

In the garden there was an old man chopping wood. He saw Mr Mean going past and called out.

"Excuse me," he called. "Could you give an old man a bit of a hand young fellow-me-lad?"

"No!" replied Mr Mean. "It's your wood. You chop it!"

But, as soon as the words had passed his lips, guess what happened?

His ears turned into tomatoes!!

"Oh no!" he gasped.

The old man chuckled.

And Mr Mean remembered the wizard's words.

"Yes! Yes!" he cried. "Of course I'll give you a hand."

And he chopped and chopped until all the wood was cut.

And the tomatoes turned back into ears, and off he went.

The old man chuckled again, and turned back into the wizard.

He was teaching Mr Mean a lesson, just as he'd promised.

Eventually Mr Mean arrived in the town.

There was a little boy crying because his ball had got stuck on top of a wall.

"Please sir," cried the boy. "Please sir, could you reach my ball down for me?"

"No!" retorted Mr Mean. "It's your ball. You . . ." Then he stopped.

There was a funny tingling feeling in his feet.

"Yes! Yes!" he said hurriedly. "Of course I will."

And he reached up and passed the ball to the boy, and went on his way, looking anxiously at his feet.

The little boy stopped crying and turned into the wizard.

"I think," he said to himself, "I think that Mr Mean, by and large, is beginning, if I'm not very much mistaken, to not be quite so mean, and, I think, although I could be wrong, although I never am, that he has, thank goodness, learned his lesson."

Today he's nothing like so mean as he used to be.

And he doesn't keep his money in a box in the kitchen any more.

He spent it all on having his house mended and painted and made spick and span.

And he's turned into quite a generous sort of a fellow.

Goodness, he's so generous, do you know what he gave his brother last Christmas?

Two pieces of coal!

MORE SPECIAL OFFERS
FOR MR MEN AND LITTLE MISS READERS

In every Mr Men and Little Miss book like this one, <u>and now</u> in the Mr Men sticker and activity books, you will find a special token. Collect six tokens and we will send you a gift of your choice
Choose either a <u>Mr Men</u> or <u>Little Miss</u> poster, **or** a Mr Men or Little Miss **double sided** full colour bedroom door hanger.

Return this page **with six tokens per gift required** to:
Marketing Dept., MM / LM, World International Ltd.,
PO Box 7, Manchester, M19 2HD

Your name:_____ Age: _____

Address: _____

_____

_____ Postcode: _____

Parent / Guardian Name (Please Print)_____

Please tape a 20p coin to your request to cover part post and package cost

I enclose <u>six</u> tokens per gift, and 20p please send me:-

Posters:- Mr Men Poster ☐ Little Miss Poster ☐

Door Hangers - Mr Nosey / Muddle ☐ Mr Greedy / Lazy ☐

Mr Tickle / Grumpy ☐ Mr Slow / Busy ☐

Mr Messy / Quiet ☐ Mr Perfect / Forgetful ☐

L Miss Fun / Late ☐ L Miss Helpful / Tidy ☐

L Miss Busy / Brainy ☐ L Miss Star / Fun ☐

Please Tick Appropriate Box

20p
Stick 20p here please

We may occasionally wish to advise you of other Mr Men gifts.
If you would rather we didn't please tick this box ☐

MR. GREEDY
ENTRANCE FEE 3 SAUSAGES

Collect six of these tokens
You will find one inside every
Mr Men and Little Miss book
which has this special offer.

1 TOKEN

Offer open to residents of UK, Channel Isles and Ireland only

Full colour Mr Men and Little Miss Library Presentation Cases in durable, wipe clean plastic.

In response to the many thousands of requests for the above, we are delighted to advise that these are now available direct from ourselves,
for only **£4.99** (inc VAT) plus 50p p&p.
The full colour boxes accommodate each complete library. They have an integral carrying handle as well as a neat stay closed fastener.
Please do not send cash in the post. Cheques should be made payable to **World International Ltd. for the sum of £5.49** (inc p&p) per box.

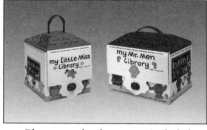

Please note books are not included.

Please return this page with your cheque, stating below which presentation box you would like, to:
Mr Men Office, World International
PO Box 7, Manchester, M19 2HD

Your name:_____

Address: _____

_____

_____Postcode: _____

Name of Parent/Guardian (please print):_____

Signature:_____

I enclose a cheque for £_____ made payable to World International Ltd.,

Please send me a Mr Men Presentation Box [   ]

Little Miss Presentation Box [   ]   (please tick or write in quantity)
and allow 28 days for delivery

Thank you

Offer applies to UK, Eire & Channel Isles only